Animal Antics

THE LEAPING LION

For George, who loves jumping too – LC
For Martha, Helen, Archie, and The Moog – PA

STRIPES PUBLISHING
An imprint of Magi Publications
1 The Coda Centre, 189 Munster Road,
London SW6 6AW

A paperback original
First published in Great Britain in 2010

Text copyright © Lucy Courtenay, 2010
Illustrations copyright © Phil Alderson, 2010

ISBN: 978-1-84715-132-2

The right of Lucy Courtenay and Phil Alderson to
be identified as the author and illustrator of this work
respectively has been asserted by them in accordance
with the Copyright, Designs and Patents Act, 1988.

Printed and bound in the UK.

10 9 8 7 6 5 4 3 2 1

Animal Antics

THE LEAPING LION

LUCY COURTENAY

Illustrated by Phil Alderson

Stripes

Animals!

Everyone loves animals. Feathery, furry, fierce. Scaly, scary, hairy. Cute, a bit smelly, all-round bonkers.

But let's be honest. How well do we really know them?
I know my dog, you might say.
I know my cat and my hamster.

Ah, I say. You may think you know them, but you DON'T.
When you watch them, they do catty
and doggy and hamstery things.
But what about when you're not watching?
Who knows what they do when you're snoozing
in your beds or when you're at school?

And what about the rest of the animal kingdom?
The world is full of amazing creatures –
from camels in the desert, to baboons
in the forest, and fish in the deepest ocean.

We know even less about them.
For all we know, they might like dancing. Or doing
handstands. Or playing thumb wars. Actually, not that
one because most animals don't have thumbs.
But you know what I mean.

Maybe we don't know animals as well as we think.
Take LIONS, for instance…

Chapter One

Brian loved to leapfrog.

He was a small lion, but he was springy. He bunched up his back legs and leaped into the air, soaring over anything in his path. He leapfrogged over his mum. He leapfrogged over his dad. He leapfrogged over his sisters and any other animals who let him. Brian was extremely good at leapfrogging, and he knew it.

Animal Antics

"I'm the best leapfrogger in the whole of Africa," he boasted one day. "I jumped over a zebra this morning."

"Waste of time jumping *over* zebras, son," said his dad, with a shake of his huge black mane. "You should be jumping *on* zebras. And eating them."

"I don't want to eat zebras," said Brian. "I just want to jump over them and feel the wind in my ears."

His dad growled. His sisters tutted. But Brian didn't care. "I'm the best leapfrogger in the WHOLE of Africa," he repeated.

"Be quiet and eat your antelope," said his mother.

Brian spent hours in the wide grassland of the African savannah, finding things to practise on. He soon discovered that leapfrogging over rocks was better than leapfrogging over zebras. Rocks didn't turn round and bite you the way zebras sometimes did. Brian leapfrogged over every rock he could find.

But soon, he needed a new challenge.

From the high red rocks where Brian lived with his family, he had a good view across the savannah. Animals roamed peacefully on all sides. Somewhere out there was the perfect leapfrog challenge and he was going to find it. Brian settled down beside his warm mother and closed his eyes.

The sun went down and the stars came out. The noises of the night were all around. But Brian was already dreaming.

Animal Antics

The next day Brian went in search of his new challenge.

He passed rocks.

"Done them," he said.

He passed zebras.

"Done them," he said.

"Done them. Done them," he added, passing warthogs and hyenas.

On he went, prowling beneath the thorn trees.

Soon he spotted Linus the leopard. Linus was halfway up a tree, sunning himself on a branch. Although Linus was much older than Brian, he was Brian's best friend. Linus was also the grumpiest leopard on the savannah.

"How are you today, Linus?" said Brian.

"Hungry," said Linus. "My paws ache from chasing yesterday's dinner. Which I *didn't* catch. And I've got a mosquito bite between my shoulders that I can't itch." He dangled one long, spotty leg over the branch. "Go away, Brian."

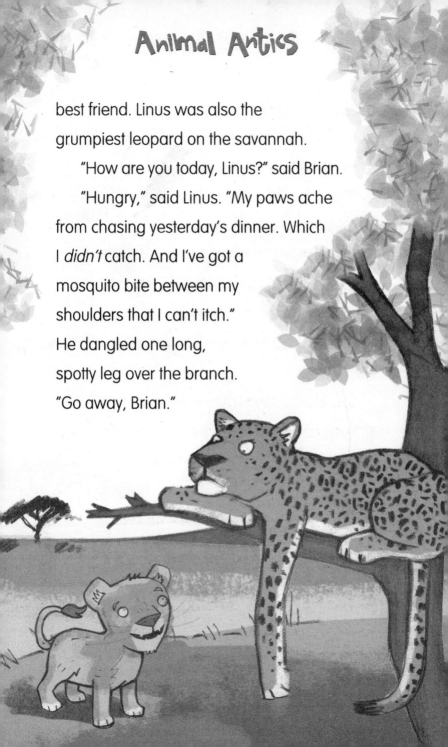

"Can I leapfrog over you?" asked Brian.

Linus blinked. "For a moment," he said, "I thought you asked if you could leapfrog over me."

"I did," said Brian.

"Which part of 'Go away' didn't you understand?" Linus asked.

Brian wasn't giving up.

"That's a nice branch you're sitting on," he said.

Linus stretched out another spotty leg so it was dangling down like the first. "It is, isn't it?" he said. "Good and high."

Brian pretended to stare very hard at the branch. "By the look of things," he said, "the fire ants like it too."

"Fire ants?" Linus stood up very fast. "I hate fire ants."

"They have a really nasty bite," said Brian.

Animal Antics

"I'd get off that branch if I were you. They're heading straight for your bottom."

Linus was about to leap off when he saw Brian smirk. He stopped, one paw in mid-air.

"Brian?" said Linus.

Brian straightened his face. "Yes, Linus?"

"You're lying about the fire ants because you want to jump over my branch," Linus growled, lying back down. "Go and annoy someone else before I bite you."

Brian sighed; his plan had failed. He left Linus and went on with his search.

The sun beat down, but Brian refused to give up.

He asked the hippos at the watering hole if he could leapfrog over them. They yawned at him, like he'd asked the most boring question in the world. He asked the baboons among the rocks. They screamed at him to get lost.

Hungry and tired, Brian was almost ready to give up.

And then he saw four thick grey legs swaying towards him through the grass.

Chapter Two

Brian looked up, and up, and up. The grey legs stretched higher than his head. After the grey legs came a huge grey tummy. A long, snakey trunk and two white tusks. And miles up in the air, two huge flapping ears.

It was Big Earl, the bull elephant.

Brian's eyes grew round. The Perfect Leapfrog Challenge!

Animal Antics

Big Earl was almost as important as Brian's dad on the savannah. Brian didn't know him very well and was a bit scared of the elephant, but he was desperate.

"Hello, Big Earl," he said, plucking up courage. "Can I leapfrog over you?"

Big Earl's voice rumbled like thunder, way over Brian's head.

"*You?*" he said. "Leapfrog over *me*?"

"Yes," said Brian. "Please?"

Big Earl laughed. "But you're a flea," he said. "You're a mouse. You're TINY. You couldn't jump over a twig."

Brian pulled himself up as tall as he could. "I'm not *that* small," he said. "And I'm the best leapfrogger in the whole of Africa. Watch!"

Brian put on his best display, and hopped over a large rock by Big Earl's feet.

"Very impressive, little lion," said Big Earl.

"Now step aside. I'm busy."

The bull elephant swiped at Brian with his trunk. Brian ducked.

"It won't take long," Brian said from behind the rock. "You won't even notice I'm doing it."

Big Earl flapped his great ears and stamped his feet. He trumpeted so loudly that the ground shook. "You're beginning to make me angry," he said. "GO AWAY."

Animal Antics

"I'll just take a little run-up," Brian went on. "It'll be over before you know it."

Big Earl stared hard at Brian. Brian stared back. The hippos at the watering hole watched. So did the baboons, and the warthogs, the hyenas and the zebras, and a gnu or two.

"Very well, pipsqueak," said Big Earl at last. "But you won't get higher than my knees."

"You're wrong," Brian said, feeling triumphant. "Watch this."

Before Big Earl could change his mind, Brian started measuring his run-up. The hippos

and the baboons, the warthogs and the
hyenas, the zebras and the gnus were still
watching.

"This is going to be hilarious!" laughed one
of the hyenas.

For the first time, Brian felt a tiny bit
anxious. Big Earl wasn't just any elephant.
He was a *bull* elephant.

He was **HUGE.**

Animal Antics

Perhaps he should have started with a smaller one.

But it was too late to back out now.

"I'm the best leapfrogger in the whole of Africa," Brian reminded himself.

He started his run-up.

"He hasn't a hope!" honked the hippos, as Brian gathered speed.

"He's bonkers!" babbled the baboons, as Brian got faster.

"Wasting his time!" warbled the warthogs, as Brian streaked towards Big Earl.

"Ours too," said the zebras, flicking their stripey tails.

"Hee hee!" the hyenas howled.

Brian tried to ignore them and think only of Big Earl. The bull elephant was looming. Any minute now, Brian would have to jump.

"He'll lose," mooed the gnus.

Brian bunched up his back legs and flung himself into the air.

UP ...
AND UUPP ...
AND UUUPPP ...
WHAM!

Brian crashed into Big Earl's bottom with a loud

"OOF!"

He slid down the elephant's long grey legs and landed in a furry heap at Big Earl's feet.

The watching animals screeched with laughter.

"I was wrong," said Big Earl with a smirk.

Brian gasped for breath. His lungs felt like two burst balloons.

"You got further than my knees," Big Earl said. "Stick to something smaller next time, squirt. A tortoise, maybe."

Brian struggled to his feet, swayed and fell over. He lay on the ground and stared up at the tuft on Big Earl's tail.

"I wouldn't stay there if I were you," said Big Earl. "Unless you want a pat on the head."

HA HA!

TEE HEE!

Chapter Three

Brian walked back to the high red rocks with his head hanging down. Animals sniggered as he passed.

"Did you see that?"

"Right into Big Earl's bottom!"

"Funniest thing I ever saw!"

Brian's mother had caught a juicy gnu for tea, but Brian wasn't hungry. He sat with his head on his paws and watched his family eat.

"Aren't you going to have some, Brian?" said his mother.

Brian shook his head.

"You can have this bit if you like," said his younger sister Diane.

Brian felt miserable. Diane worshipped him. He didn't want her to know what a fool he'd been.

"You're not turning into a *vegetarian*, are you?" said Leanne, his older sister.

Brian blushed with shame. Leanne already thought he was a fool … and he hated the fact that he'd just proved his older sister right.

"First you jump over zebras," said his dad. "Now you pooh-pooh gnu. What's wrong, son? Try biting the next zebra you see. You'll feel better in no time."

"Why don't we have a game of leapfrog

after dinner?" said his mum.

"No!" Brian shouted. "I'm never leapfrogging over anything EVER AGAIN!"

And he ran away to mope under a thorn tree for the rest of the evening.

I guess I'm not the best leapfrogger in the whole of Africa after all, he thought sadly to himself.

How could he have got it so wrong?

I'll never leapfrog again, Brian vowed. *Never, never, never.*

Brian carried on moping for the next two days.

"Chin up, son," said his dad helplessly. "That's three days in a row you haven't eaten your gazelle."

"What's the matter, Brian?" asked Diane.

"Who cares," said Leanne, rolling her eyes.

Animal Antics

Brian gazed into the distance. His disastrous leapfrog would be all round the savannah by now. Everyone would be laughing at him. Him! The King of the Savannah's son! How could he bear the embarrassment?

After a week, Brian's mother got so worried that she suggested something extraordinary.

"Why don't you come on a buffalo hunt with me and your sisters?"

Brian couldn't believe his ears. "Me?" he said. "Go on a hunt? Girls go hunting, not boys!"

"Boys hunt too," said Diane. "Sometimes."

"Is it dangerous?" Brian asked.

His older sister laughed. "You're not scared, are you?"

"No," said Brian, glaring at her. "I've never hunted before, that's all."

His dad's tummy rumbled. "Make up your

mind, son," he said. "I'm getting hungry. Are you going or not?"

Brian thought about it. Hunts always looked like fun. Maybe he could forget about leapfrog and be good at hunting instead. He felt better already.

"Those buffalo better watch out!" he said.

His mother looked relieved. "That's more like it. We'll go to Big Gap Gully. They have lovely juicy ones up there."

It was a day's walk to Big Gap Gully. Brian's dad led the way, swinging his head and sniffing the air. Although he wouldn't be hunting, it was useful having him along. Brian listened to his mum and sisters talking about great hunts they'd been on in the past. He was starting to feel excited.

"Do you remember the three-legged gnu?"

"And when we got two antelopes at once?"

"And Mum chasing off those vultures?"

They passed a herd of zebras. Once Brian would have leapfrogged over every one. But not today. His excitement about the hunt died away, and instead he started to feel scared.

What if he was as bad at hunting as he was at leapfrog?

The family stopped at the watering hole for a drink. Brian's heart sank when he saw Chester the cheetah at the water's edge. Chester was a gossip and knew everything that happened on the savannah. He was bound to know about Big Earl.

"Seen any elephants lately, Brian?" Chester chortled.

"What's he talking about?" said Diane.

"Nothing," said Brian.

"Didn't he tell you?" said Chester. "He tried to jump over Big Earl and crashed into his—"

"Shut up," said Brian, as Chester started giggling.

Brian's dad loomed over Chester. "Do you find my son amusing?" he growled.

Chester's spots went pale. "O-o-of course not, your Kingliness," he stuttered. "It was j-j-just a little joke." And he slunk away.

Brian breathed a sigh of relief. It was useful having a dad everyone was afraid of. But as he had a drink, he couldn't ignore the way his family was looking at him.

"Everything all right, son?" said his dad.

"You'd tell us if something was wrong, wouldn't you?" said his mum.

"We won't laugh," Diane said.

"Not much, anyway," said Leanne.

"I'm fine," said Brian, not feeling fine at all. "Can we go to Big Gap Gully now?"

Chapter Four

After several hours' walking, they reached a wide patch of grassland.

"Here we are," said Brian's dad, stretching out on a warm rock. "Big Gap Gully."

Brian looked around. He could see the deep gash in the ground that gave Big Gap Gully its name. Buffalo were grazing in groups near the gully's edge.

Animal Antics

Brian's dad yawned and settled down for a spot of sunbathing. "Let me know when dinner's ready," he said.

"Right," said Brian's mother. "Copy me and your sisters, Brian. Snuggle your tummy close to the ground and creep along like a caterpillar. That's it."

Brian did as he was told. He could see the buffalo through the stalks of grass. He shuffled forward very slowly.

One of the buffalo suddenly sniffed the air. "Lions!" it bellowed.

The buffalo scattered. Some went left. Others went right. The sound of their thundering hooves was deafening.

"Bri-an!" screeched Leanne. "Was that you? The buffalo never smell us normally."

"No!" Brian said. "Why is everything always *my* fault?"

Animal Antics

"Stop arguing and CHASE THEM!" roared
Brian's mother.

Brian jumped up. There were buffalo
everywhere. He didn't know which way to run.

"They're getting away!" his older sister
shouted. "After them, Brian, you idiot!"

Brian decided to follow the largest buffalo he could see. It was running straight towards Big Gap Gully. Brian speeded up, determined to catch it.

Up ahead, the buffalo leaped over the gully. It stumbled as it reached the far side and fell to its knees.

"Jump, Brian!" yelled Diane. "The buffalo's down. Jump and you'll catch it!"

Jump? Over Big Gap Gully?

Suddenly all Brian could think about was Big Earl's large grey bottom. He panicked. He was going to fall down the gully and hurt himself! He dug in his paws and slithered to a halt at the edge of the ravine.

The buffalo couldn't believe its luck as it scrambled to its feet.

"Loser!" it shouted, and ran off to join the rest of its herd.

"What do you mean, it could be worse?" said Brian to Linus the next day, as they lay under a thorn tree. "It's my fault we had no dinner last night. I've been sent home in disgrace. None of my family is talking to me. And a buffalo called me a loser. That's pretty bad, Linus."

"It's not as bad as the time I fell out of a tree and squashed my uncle Len," said the leopard. "Or the time I got my tail caught in Crosby's mouth."

This got Brian's attention. "Crosby the crocodile?" he said. "And you escaped? I don't believe you."

"What do you think I am?" said Linus. "A ghost?"

"I never heard of anyone escaping from Crosby before," said Brian.

Animal Antics

Linus almost smiled. "There's always a first time."

"Why are you in such a good mood today, Linus?" Brian asked, looking sideways at his friend. "You're never in a good mood."

"What can I say?" said Linus. "Other people's misery cheers me up."

Animal Antics

"It's more than that," said Brian. "I can tell."

Linus grinned, showing his pointed teeth. "Maybe it's because I've heard something," he said. He stood up and stretched his long, spotty body.

Brian forgot about his terrible buffalo hunt. "What?"

"Nothing you'll be interested in."

"How do you know?" Brian said. "I might be *very* interested."

Linus eyed the branches of the thorn tree. "I'm off for a snooze," he said. "See you later, Brian."

Brian shot out a paw as Linus prepared to jump, pinning the leopard's tail to the ground. Linus tumbled back with a yowl.

"Let go!"

"Start talking, Linus," said Brian. "Or Crosby won't be the only animal to bite your tail."

Chapter Five

Linus wriggled, but Brian held him firmly.

"I just heard something interesting from two warthogs as they were walking under my tree yesterday," the leopard said. "That's all."

"What did they say?" asked Brian.

"I can't remember the *exact* details," said Linus.

Animal Antics

Brian pressed harder. "Where can I find these warthogs?" he said. "I'll ask them myself."

"You can't," Linus said. He patted his tummy with a heavy paw. "Warthogs should know better than to walk under trees with leopards in them. Let go of my tail, will you, Brian?"

"I'll let go when you start talking," said Brian.

"OK, OK," said Linus. "If you must know, the Animal Olympics are coming."

Brian let go. At once, Linus leaped into the branches of the thorn tree and started licking his tail.

"Animal Olympics?" Brian said. "Here, on the savannah? When?"

"Three weeks," Linus said, moving on to his ears.

A thousand thoughts rushed into Brian's head. He could enter something. He could win. His family would forgive him for losing that buffalo. The animals at the watering hole would never tease him again.

"Do you know the list of events?" Brian asked.

"The warthogs mentioned a couple of things," said Linus. He scratched himself under the chin. "The Sprint. The One-Leg Balance. The River Swim with crocodile hazards."

"I can't do those," said Brian, feeling disappointed. "Anything else?"

Linus hesitated. "Leapfrog," he said.

Brian's heart thumped. "I don't do leapfrog any more."

"Shame," said Linus. "You used to be the best leapfrogger in the whole of Africa. Didn't you?"

Brian left Linus in the thorn tree. His head was buzzing. He really wanted to enter the

Animal Antics

Animal Olympics and win an orchid crown. But he'd vowed to stop leapfrogging for ever.

There was a small rock lying nearby. Brian ran at it very slowly and jumped. The wind whistled in his ears as he landed on the other side. He'd forgotten how lovely leapfrogging was.

Could he really do it again?

BOING!

Animal Antics

Back at the high red rocks, Brian found his family tucking into a juicy buffalo.

"You caught one, then," he said.

"No thanks to you," said Leanne.

Brian was starving. He eyed the buffalo hungrily. "Any left for me?"

"Sorry," said Diane, looking upset. "You should have got here earlier."

"Have some of mine, Brian," his mother said.

Brian sat beside his mother and nibbled a bit of buffalo. "I'm sorry I let you all down at Big Gap Gully," he said. "I've had a bit of trouble with jumping over things lately."

"Is that because of Big Earl?" asked his mother.

"Chester said you crashed into him,"

Leanne said. She started laughing. "I would have *loved* to see that."

"Don't tease him," said Diane, making Leanne laugh even more.

Brian told his family the whole story, trying to ignore Leanne, who was now laughing like a hyena.

"You landed on an elephant's bum and you didn't bite it?" his dad said. "I'll never understand you, son."

"The thing is," Brian said, "the Animal Olympics are coming to the savannah and there's a Leapfrog event. I've decided to take up leapfrogging again because I want to win."

Brian's mother gasped. His dad drummed the ground with his great paws. Diane gave a whoop. News of the Animal Olympics even made Leanne sit up. Brian's sisters both – yes, *both* – smiled at him. His mum and dad smiled at him. It was a wonderful feeling.

"Imagine an Animal Olympics orchid crown winner in our family!" said his mother proudly. "Have some buffalo liver, Brian. You need to build up your strength!"

The next morning, everyone was talking about the Animal Olympics down at the watering hole.

"Sprint, Sprint, Sprint!" yelled Chester the cheetah, racing through a group of flamingos. "I'm gonna win the Sprint, Sprint, Sprint!"

"It's the River Swim for me," said Graham the gnu to one of his gnu friends. "I'm awfully good at swimming."

Animal Antics

"I *will* look forward to that," said Crosby the crocodile from the water, making Graham run up the bank in fright.

"Excuse me. How do I enter the Animal Olympics?" Brian asked a group of chatting gazelles.

The gazelles took a step back. They didn't like lions very much.

"Talk to Otis the ostrich, not us," said the bravest gazelle. "He's by the mud baths."

"Form a LINE!" shouted Otis, as the animals jostled for position. "Name? Species? Number of legs? Event?"

"Brian," said Brian, when he made it to the front. "Lion. Four legs. Leapfrog."

There was a hush. Brian held his head high.

"Brian's entering the Leapfrog!" Chester

Animal Antics

sang into the silence. "Oh, tum-tee-tum-tee-tum, watch out for the elephant's bum, Oh, tum-tee-tum-tee-tum…"

"You can finish your song when I've won," Brian shot at Chester.

Two flamingos clapped their wings approvingly at Brian's rhyme.

"I didn't think I'd see *you* here, Brian," said Linus, coming up to Brian as Chester flounced away. "Have you entered something?"

"The Leapfrog," said Brian.

Linus whistled. "That's a surprise," he said. "I'm doing the Sprint. I can run quite fast when I want to. Who are you going to practise on?"

"You?" Brian asked hopefully.

"No," said Linus.

"Rocks, then," said Brian.

"Ask Gina the giraffe," said Linus. "You have to aim high if you want to win an orchid crown."

"I aimed high with Big Earl," said Brian, "and look what happened."

But Linus's words made Brian think.

Perhaps he *would* have a chat with Gina the giraffe after all.

Having a chat with Gina wasn't easy.

"I don't want to eat you, Gina," said Brian, for the hundredth time.

Gina the giraffe was standing behind a thick thorn bush. "Of course you want to eat me," she said. "Lions eat giraffes. It's what you do."

"Not me," said Brian. "I just want to jump over you."

Animal Antics

Gina moved further behind the thorn bush. Her big brown eyes gazed down at Brian. "And then you'll sink your claws and your teeth into my back," she said. "And pull me over and eat me."

"Gina," said Brian, "how can I make you believe me?"

"Turn into a warthog," said Gina. "Then I'll believe you."

Brian sighed. Sometimes he wished he wasn't a lion. Lions didn't deserve their reputation for eating everything that moved. OK, maybe his dad did. But Brian wasn't his dad.

He left Gina alone and went looking for some bigger rocks. He'd only been practising for three days, and already most of the rocks on the savannah were too small. But after a while, he gave up. Linus was right. He was never going to get good enough for the Animal Olympics by practising on rocks.

He went back to the thorn bush again, but Gina had wandered off. Brian put his nose to the ground and followed her trail through the grass and down to the watering hole.

For once, the watering hole was quiet. Gina stood at the edge with her legs splayed out wide, having a drink. Brian's heart skipped a beat. Gina was even more perfect for leapfrog practice than he'd thought. He could start with her down low, like she was right now. Then, when he could do that, he'd ask her to straighten her legs a bit. Then a bit more.

That's where I went wrong with Big Earl, he thought.

Brian cleared his throat, not wanting to scare her, and padded forward. Gina squealed with fright. But not because of Brian.

Animal Antics

Crosby the crocodile was lunging out of the water towards her with his jaws open wide.

Chapter seven

Brian didn't hesitate. He raced to the edge of the water and stood between Crosby and Gina.

"Back off, Crosby," he growled.

Crosby landed with a wet flop on the muddy shore in front of Brian. He was twice as long as Brian, and had four times as many teeth. He snapped his jaws. "Get out of my way. The giraffe is mine. Or would you prefer me to eat you instead?"

But Brian stood his ground. *If Linus got away from Crosby,* Brian told himself, *I can too.* "No," he said. "She's mine. I saw her first. Didn't I, Gina?"

"I don't want *either* of you to eat me," Gina wailed.

"I'm not going to eat you," Brian reminded the giraffe.

"Ha, ha, ha!" laughed Crosby, making Gina wail even louder. "You are very funny, little lion. Now GET OUT OF MY WAY."

Brian sprang forward and clamped his jaws around Crosby's nose, bringing the crocodile's teeth together with a snap. Crosby's mud-coloured eyes bulged in shock.

"Mmphdmph!" Crosby mumbled.

Animal Antics

Brian knew it was rude to talk with his mouth full, so he opened his jaws and let Crosby go. "Go and find someone else to eat," he said. "Or next time it won't be your nose that gets it."

"You bit me!" said Crosby in astonishment.

"And I'll bite you again if I have to," said Brian. "This giraffe is *mine*."

"You'll regret this," Crosby hissed. "I'll be back when you least expect it. And *I'll* be the one doing the biting."

He slid back into the water with a lash of his great scaly tail, leaving behind a line of furious ripples.

When he was sure Crosby had gone, Brian turned round to see if Gina was all right.

"You're really *not* going to eat me?" the giraffe said, her legs trembling.

"No," said Brian. "I'm not."

"You saved me from Crosby and you're not

going to eat me," Gina said in wonder. "I never thought I'd say this to a lion … but I think you're fantastic, Brian. You can jump over me as much as you like."

Brian beamed. "Thanks, Gina!"

"We'd better start straight away," said Gina. "The Animal Olympics begin in just two weeks!"

The next fortnight passed in a blur.

Brian practised leapfrogging over Gina every spare moment. Each day, Gina straightened her legs a little more and made herself a bit taller. And by the end of every day, Brian was sailing over Gina and hardly touching her back with his paws at all. Brian tried to persuade Leanne to enter the Leapfrog as well, but his big sister snorted and told him she wasn't a cricket.

Animal Antics

On the day before the Animal Olympics were due to begin, the whole family came to watch Brian training.

"That giraffe lets you jump over her every day, son?" said Brian's dad, staring at Gina.

"Yes," said Brian.

"And you never bite her?" his dad asked, still staring. A bit of dribble appeared in the corner of his mouth.

"No," said Brian.

"Not even the teensiest bit?" The dribble ran down the big lion's sharp teeth and hit the ground with a splat.

"I've got a lovely bit of gazelle for dinner later," said Brian's mum loudly. "Think about that instead of the giraffe, dear."

Brian's dad put his great head on his paws and tried not to look at Gina.

"Today's the big one," said Brian. "Gina's going to stand up straight for the first time. If I can jump over her, then I think I'm ready for the Animal Olympics."

"Go, Brian!" shouted Diane, as Brian took his run-up.

"Go, Brian the flea!" Leanne yelled, as Brian flew over Gina's back like a furry golden bird.

"Is that a compliment?" Brian asked, grinning with pride as he got his breath back.

"Yes," said Leanne. "Fleas jump like crazy. They are also very annoying and small. It describes you perfectly."

Gina stood a safe distance away from Brian's dad. "I can stand on a rock if you want to go higher, Brian," she said.

He shook his head. "Thanks, Gina, but I'm as ready as I'm going to be," he said.

"No offence," said Gina, giving Brian's dad one last nervous glance, "but please, never bring your dad to watch us train again."

Chapter Eight

The sun rose like a giant red ball on the day of the Animal Olympics.

Hundreds of events were taking place across the whole of Africa. There was Tree Swinging and Swamp Swimming in the jungle areas. Cliff Leaping and Dragging Prey Uphill in the mountains. Sand Racing and Dune Sliding in the deserts.

Animal Antics

"I didn't know so many different animals lived here," said Diane in wonder, as Brian and his family watched hundreds of beasts and birds heading for the watering hole where the savannah events were taking place.

"I've never seen one of those before," said his mother, as a large stripey antelope galloped past.

"Do you think they're nice to eat?" said his dad.

"Brian's getting nervous," teased Leanne, glancing at Brian pacing up and down the high red rocks. "Aren't you, Brian?"

"No," said Brian with a gulp.

The lions strolled down to the watering hole with Brian's dad leading the way. All the animals dived out of their path, keen to keep their distance.

Animal Antics

Brian saw Linus talking to two terrified warthogs.

"Hi, Linus," he said. "Ready for the Sprint?"

Linus looked round. The warthogs saw their chance and ran away. "I'm not doing it," he said. "I ate too much last night. Running will give me indigestion."

Brian looked at Linus's tummy. It was enormous. "What's in there?" he said. "A hippo?"

"I heard that," said a nearby hippo, swaying her large bottom crossly.

Linus shook his head. "I ate a cousin of those warthogs I was talking to. *That* was a tricky conversation."

Chester the cheetah dashed up and stopped in front of Linus with a sneer.

"Hey, Fatso," he said. "I hear you're entering the Sprint? Well, you can join my dots

Animal Antics

– but you gotta catch me first!"

The cheetah shot off again, knocking a
gazelle into the watering hole.

"Now that's put me in a *really* bad mood," said Linus.

"Chester's been teasing me for weeks about Big Earl," said Brian. "If I can ignore him, so can you. Enter the race, Linus. Do it to annoy him."

Linus shook his head. "I'm not entering," he said in a final-sounding voice. "I'm here to see you do the Leapfrog, and that's that."

"Suit yourself," said Brian. He gazed out at the river that fed the watering hole. It was thick and fast-flowing at this time of year, its surface covered with long brown logs. One of the logs yawned and snapped its teeth.

"Conditions are perfect for the River Swim," he said, changing the subject.

"Perfect for the crocodiles," Linus agreed.

"The crocodile hazards are too close together," complained Graham the gnu. "It's a disgrace."

Animal Antics

The other gnu competitors agreed loudly.
"We won't stand a chance!"

"The crocs outnumber us two to one!"

"We don't give away orchid crowns," said
Otis the ostrich. "You have to *earn* them."

Seeing the crocodile hazards made Brian
think of Crosby. He remembered the
crocodile's last words with a sudden shiver.

I'll be back when you least expect it.

Animal Antics

All those times Brian had been at the watering hole … Crosby could have eaten him. How could he have forgotten Crosby's promise? Brian glanced around, feeling nervous. Perhaps he was in the crowd. Perhaps he would jump on him at any moment.

A trumpeting sound made Brian start. Big Earl was standing beside a gnu on the far side of the watering hole. The elephant gave a final trumpet and the chattering animals fell silent.

"Thank you, Big Earl," said Otis. "I'm pleased to declare the Animal Olympics OPEN!"

Everyone honked, growled, squeaked and bellowed with excitement. Brian tried to roar, but his throat was dry. His eyes darted from left to right.

Where are you, Crosby? he thought.

Animal Antics

"The first event will be the One-Leg Balance," said Otis. "Second, the Sprint. Third, the River Swim. Fourth, the Jumping Straight Up In The Air. And fifth, the Leapfrog. All competitors for the One-Leg Balance, please follow me!"

Animal Antics

Everyone followed the ostrich to the Thorniest Thorn Tree on the far bank of the watering hole. Brian pushed and jostled along with the crowd, staying well away from the water's edge in case Crosby jumped out.

"This will be a fair contest," Otis told the six flamingos jogging on the spot beneath the Thorniest Thorn Tree. "No pushing, pecking or distracting. On your marks… GO!"

The flamingos snapped up one leg each and stood very still. A hush fell across the watching crowd.

"Is it me," said Linus, "or are there six flamingos and seven legs?"

"Third flamingo from the left!" shouted Otis. "You are still standing on both feet. Disqualified!"

Chapter Nine

Twenty minutes later, five flamingos were still standing exactly where they had started. The crowd started yawning.

"This is boring," said Linus. "Let's go and watch the Sprint."

"Maybe we should practise *your* Sprint," said Brian, following the leopard away from the Thorniest Thorn Tree.

Animal Antics

Linus looked sulky. "I told you, I'm not doing it."

"OK, up to you," said Brian, smiling to himself. He'd just had the perfect idea to make Linus change his mind. He backed away. "But you really are a fat and lazy leopard, Linus."

Linus's hackles rose. He took a step forward. "Come here and say that," he said.

Brian started to run. "You should enter a Fat and Heavy event!" he called over his shoulder. "Or a Hippo Eating contest!"

"You cheeky cub!" Linus shouted, giving chase. "I've *eaten* things for less than that!"

Brian was now running as fast as he could. Linus's legs were longer than his. It wouldn't be long before Linus caught him.

"Come and get me, Chubby!" Brian yelled.

Brian felt Linus's paws on his shoulders. He fell to the ground with Linus on top of him.

GROWL!

"Who," growled Linus, "are you calling CHUBBY?"

"How's your indigestion?" said Brian, panting and grinning at the same time.

"It's—" Linus stopped. "It's gone," he said in astonishment.

"See?" said Brian. "You *can* run. The Sprint is about to start. You're not going to let Chester win, are you?"

"That spotty little twit?" said Linus, letting go of Brian. "Of course not. I'll show that skinny kitten who's the fastest on the savannah."

Animal Antics

The Sprint was the most popular event in the whole Animal Olympics. Brian counted three antelopes, two giraffes, a hyena, two ostriches, a baboon and Chester the cheetah lining up under the thorn trees.

Linus joined the other competitors. Chester looked annoyed.

"What are *you* doing here, Fatso?" he said. "I thought you quit?"

"I'm here to join your dots," said Linus with a soft growl.

"On your marks," said Otis. "G—"

Chester shot away in a stripey streak.

"—O," finished the ostrich.

"Done it!" Chester yelled from the finishing line. "I'm the champ!"

The cheetah burst into a rude dance,

Animal Antics

wiggling his spotty bottom at the other runners
who were still charging down the track. The
crowd started muttering.

"The cheetah cheated."

"All cheetahs are cheats."

Linus burst across the line in second place.
Or – was it first?

"Give it to the leopard!" Brian shouted, as the other competitors flew over the line after Linus. "Li-NUS! Li-NUS! Li-NUS!"

The crowd took up Brian's chant. "Li-NUS! Li-NUS!" they yelled.

Otis strode up to the finishing line and pecked the cheetah hard on the nose.

"Ow!" Chester howled.

"That's for running off before I'd finished saying GO," said Otis. "The winner of the Sprint is – Linus the leopard!"

The River Swim was the next event. Brian walked with Linus to the water's edge to watch the gnus stretching their muscles and testing the water with their hooves. Everyone cheered as Linus walked past.

Animal Antics

"I told you I could do it, Brian," said Linus. He adjusted his orchid crown with one paw.

"Whatever you say, Linus." Brian stared at the water. He'd managed to forget about Crosby for a while with the excitement of the Sprint. Now thoughts of the crocodile slithered back into his mind.

Ten crocodiles were waiting for the River Swim to begin. Brian prayed that one of them was Crosby. If Crosby was in the river, Brian was safe – for the moment.

The nearest crocodile snapped its teeth. One of the gnus burst into tears and was led away from the water's edge. The rest got ready to swim for their lives.

"On your marks…" Otis shouted. "GO!"

The crowd's cheers were deafening as the gnus plunged in.

"Go GNUS, go GNUS, go GNUS!"

Brian's heart ping-ponged as the crocodiles all snapped at the speeding gnus – and missed. None of them was Crosby. Crosby had never missed a gnu in his life.

"Go GNUS, go GNUS, go GNUS!"

Graham the gnu was the first out of the water. The crowd roared as he got his orchid crown. Brian cheered as loudly as he could, but inside he was terrified.

If Crosby wasn't in the river, he could be anywhere.

And Brian was in a *lot* of trouble.

Chapter Ten

"Stop worrying about Crosby, Brian," said Linus.

"He wants me for lunch, Linus," said Brian. "He's here, watching me. I can feel it."

They passed the Thorniest Thorn Tree on their way to the Jumping Straight Up In The Air event. The five flamingos competing in the One-Leg Balance were still there. Two of them had fallen asleep.

"I got away from Crosby," Linus said. "Remember that."

Brian sighed. "Thanks, Linus," he said. "I'll try."

The Jumping Straight Up In The Air event was about to begin. Seven gazelles were bouncing from side to side, breathing deeply as they prepared to jump.

"On your marks…" said Otis. "GO!"

The gazelles leaped straight up into the air. All seven banged their heads on the overhanging branch of a thorn tree. All seven fell to the ground in a clatter of hooves and horns. No one moved.

"The Jumping Straight Up In The Air event is cancelled," Otis said, staring at the heap of gazelles. "Next!"

"That'll be the Leapfrog," said Linus, as the disappointed crowd moved away.

Animal Antics

Brian's heart skipped a beat. He didn't know which was worse: the thought of Crosby, or the thought of not winning the orchid crown in the Leapfrog.

"You can do it, Brian," said Linus. "Same as I did."

"As long as Crosby doesn't get me first," said Brian.

Brian's family was waiting for him at the Leapfrog, which was taking place beside the river.

"Good luck, Brian," said his mum. She nudged Brian's dad, who was looking over his shoulder at the heap of gazelles still lying on the grass.

"What?" said his dad, looking round. "Oh, yes. Good luck, son."

Animal Antics

"You'll be brilliant," said Diane.

"Don't embarrass us, will you?" said Leanne with a sigh.

Brian checked one last time for Crosby. Then he went to join the other four competitors – all antelopes – who were practising on some nearby rocks.

"Jumps, take your places," said Otis. "Competitors will start with the smallest animal and work their way up to the biggest."

Four different-sized animals stood in a line. Brian wanted to cheer. Warthog – easy. Zebra – peasy. Buffalo – lemon. And giraffe – squeezy! He could do this. He could!

Suddenly there was a commotion and Big Earl came swaying through the crowd, flicking his grey tail.

"Sorry I'm late," said the bull elephant, taking his place at the end of the line.

Animal Antics

"Oh no," said Brian at the sight of the bull elephant. "No, no, no!"

Of ALL the animals on the savannah! It wasn't fair!

As the first antelope ran at the warthog, Brian ran the other way. A spotty paw landed on his shoulder.

"Where are you going?" said Linus.

Animal Antics

The crowd cheered as the first antelope fell at the giraffe. The second antelope took his run-up.

"I can't jump over Big Earl," said Brian in despair.

"You made me do the Sprint," said Linus, giving him a push. "Now I'm going to make you do the Leapfrog."

The second antelope landed on the zebra. The crowd booed.

"I WON'T DO IT," Brian shouted.

"You think Crosby's the only one with teeth around here?" Linus snarled.

There was another cheer as the third antelope crashed into the buffalo. No one had even got as far as Big Earl yet. The bull elephant swished his trunk and gazed at the sky.

Brian didn't like the look of Linus's fangs.

"OK," he said, his voice trembling. "I'll do it. But if it all goes wrong, I'm blaming YOU, Linus."

The fourth antelope flew over the warthog, then the zebra, then the buffalo. There was a gasp as the antelope made it over the giraffe. Brian closed his eyes as the antelope thumped into Big Earl's legs and fell to the ground.

It was his turn.

He thought about how brave Gina had

Animal Antics

been, letting him practise on her. He thought about making his family proud again. He thought about Linus getting away from Crosby. And he started to run.

He made it over the warthog without taking a breath. The zebra's mane tickled his tummy as he flew over it. The buffalo panicked and fell to its knees, making it the easiest jump yet. Brian speeded up and soared towards the giraffe, standing tall on its four long legs. His paws touched lightly on the giraffe's back, and he was over.

Animal Antics

The noise from the crowd was deafening. Now only Big Earl stood between Brian and the orchid crown. Brian didn't let himself think too hard. He prepared to hurl himself into the air with all his might…

Suddenly, Crosby exploded out of the river in a tornado of scales and glinting teeth.

"Revenge is mine, little lion!" he shouted, and closed his jaws on Brian's tail.

The crowd screamed.

"OW!" roared Brian.

The pain gave him wings. Muscles Brian didn't know he had fired him into the air like a cannon ball. Crosby was flung sideways, back into the river with a terrible SPLASH!

UP ... UUPP ... UUUPPP ... and OVER Big Earl went Brian.

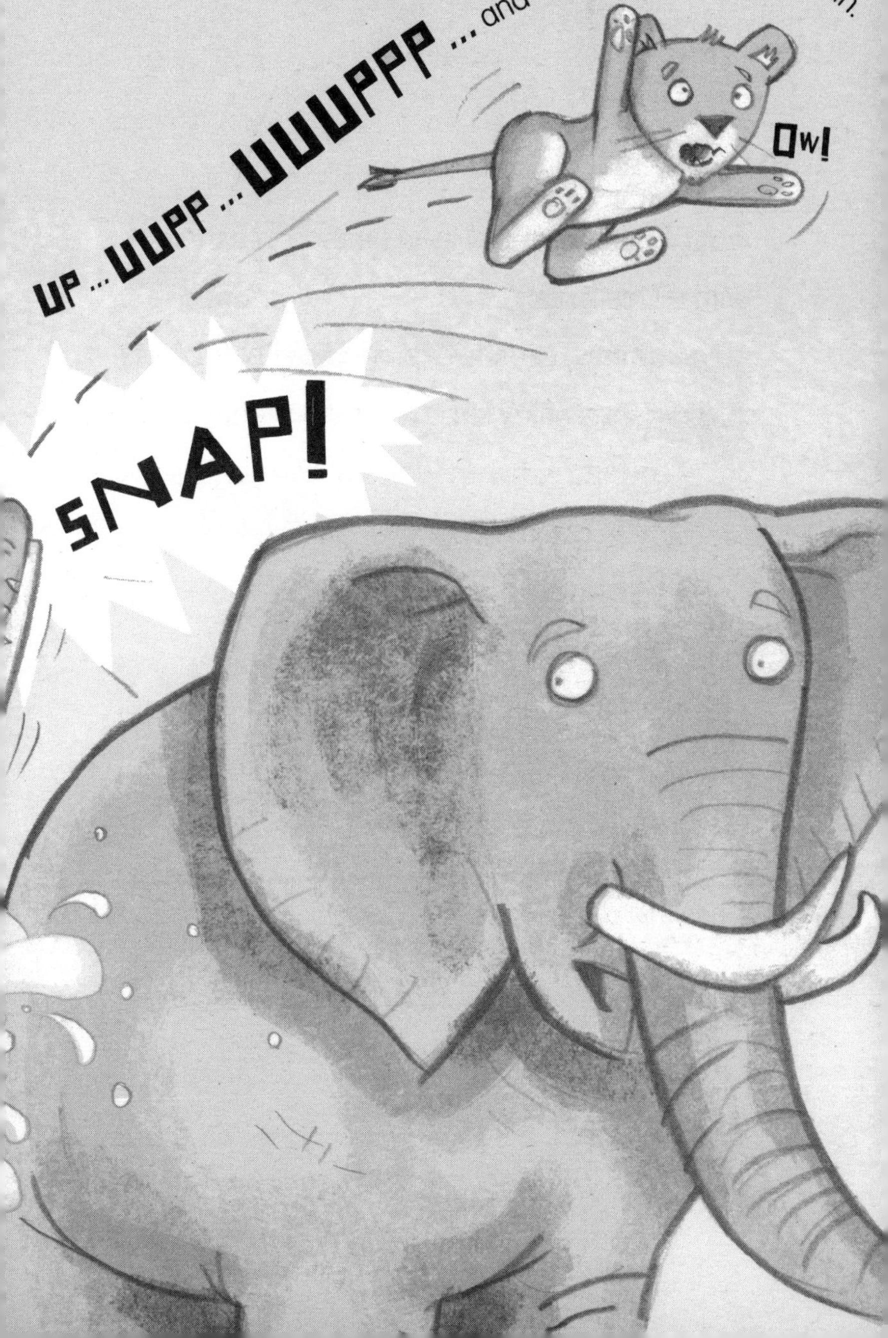

Just a bit left...

Brian couldn't stop smiling as everyone congratulated him. His parents had their paws wrapped tightly round his neck in a double hug, almost knocking the orchid crown off his head. Tears of joy streaked down Diane's furry face. Leanne's mouth was still hanging open.

"It was all thanks to you, Linus," he shouted over the noise.

"Forget it," said Linus, waving a paw.

"I got away from Crosby," yelled Brian, still finding it hard to believe. "Just like you did!"

"I never got away from Crosby," said Linus. "I just said that to stop you moaning. Crosby got my uncle Len's tail, not mine. And not just his tail, come to think of it…"

And a bit more...

The sun went down over the tired but happy savannah. The Animal Olympics were over. All the orchid crowns were won.

Well, most of them.

"My leg's killing me," said one of the five flamingos still standing under the Thorniest Thorn Tree. "Can we call it a draw?"

THE END

Totally True

Girl lions do most of the hunting.

Giraffes can nearly do the splits.

A million gnus swim across crocodile-infested rivers every year.

Not quite as many swim back again.

Gazelles can jump between four and five metres straight up in the air.

Flamingos can stand on one leg for up to four hours.

Lions ALWAYS bite the things they jump on.